OUTLAWS of the MARSH

Vol. 04

OUTLAWS of the MARSH

Vol. 04

Rags to Riches

Created by WEI DONG CHEN

Wei Dong Chen is a highly acclaimed artist and an influential leader in the "New Chinese Cartoon" trend. He is the founder of Creator World, the largest comics studio in China. His spirited and energetic work has attracted many students to his tutelage. He has published more than 300 cartoons in several countries and gained both recognition and admirers across Asia, Europe, and the USA. Mr. Chen's work is serialized in several publications, and he continues to explore new dimensions of the graphic medium.

Illustrated by XIAO LONG LIANG

Xiao Long Liang is considered one of Wei Dong Chen's greatest students. One of the most highly regarded cartoonists in China today, Xiao Long's fantastic technique and expression of Chinese culture have won him the acclaim of cartoon lovers throughout China.

Original Story
"The Water Margin" by Shi, Nai An

Editing & Designing
Mybloomy, Jonathan Evans, KH Lee, YK Kim,
HJ Lee, JS Kim, Lampin, Qing Shao, Xiao Nan Li, Ke Hu

ZHI YANG

Zhi Yang is a former government official who served under Qiu Gao. But when a shipment of goods under his command is lost, Zhi Yang is stripped of his office and cast out of the capital. When desperate times force Zhi Yang to take desperate action, he finds himself on the wrong side of the law. But a second chance comes in the form of public support and the sympathies of a powerful man.

GAI CHAO

Gai Chao lives in the village of DongQi, and is known for his generosity toward and sympathy for those less fortunate than he. When word spreads that a shipment of gold is headed toward DongQi, he is the only one man the local bandits turn to for support in planning a heist.

YONG WU

Yong Wu, also known as Wisdom Star, was once a schoolmaster and is now a respected elder in DongQi. When Gai Chao learns of the gold shipment headed their way, he enlists Yong Wu to help put together a group of men to relieve the traveling caravan of its riches.

TANG LIU

Tang Liu, also known as Red Devil, is a nomad who learns of a gold shipment out of BeiJing and immediately seeks to persuade Gai Chao to help him steal the loot. Tang Liu is a gifted fighter, but he is also impulsive and has a short temper.

SHENG GONGSUN

Sheng Gongsun is a Taoist guru also known as Cloud Dragon. Rumor has it he can manipulate the weather, but right now Sheng Gongsun only wishes to do one thing: steal the gold coming out of BeiJing.

THE RUAN BROTHERS

The Ruan Brothers are fishermen who live in the village of ShiJie, not far from LiangShan Marsh. The brothers have fallen on hard times, which make them easy targets for Yong Wu, who offers them a chance to take part in an impending heist.

LIANGSHAN MARSH

LiangShan Marsh is located near the foot of Mount Liang, in the ShanDong District of eastern China. The top of Mount Liang sits roughly 650 feet above sea level, and the Marsh is known for its thick fog, which makes navigating the waters treacherous. The fog also acts as a natural cloak that hides those who dwell within the marsh. It is here where many of the 108 spirits and fiends, brought to life in the form of outlaws and bandits, have taken refuge from those who govern China. Some have come to LiangShan after committing legitimate crimes; others have come because government corruption has driven them from their homes.

Chapter 1

The Blue-Faced Beast

Summary

Zhi Yang has returned to DongJing, hoping to restore his official position. But he is tossed out of the palace by Qiu Gao, and must sell his family's precious sword just to make the rent. While out trying to find a buyer, Zhi Yang is approached by Er Niu, a drunken thug who terrorizes the locals. Er Niu says he's interested in buying the sword, but makes unreasonable demands of Zhi Yang. Tensions escalate until the confrontation gets physical, and Zhi Yang kills Er Niu. But rather than flee, Zhi Yang turns himself in to the authorities. The citizens of DongJing rally to support him, and he is given a lenient sentence for his crime.

While being sentenced in BeiJing, Zhi Yang meets and earns the favor of Secretary Liang, who commissions him to join the local army. Zhi Yang continues to earn greater favor with Secretary Liang, and is put in charge of a very important mission…

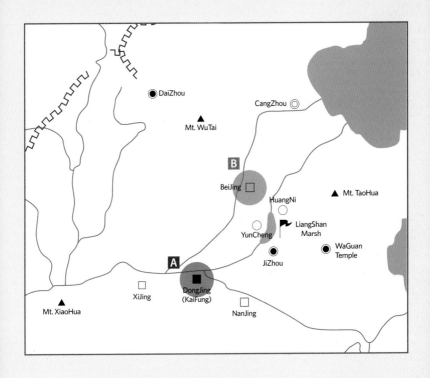

A Zhi Yang returns to DongJing to beg for reinstatement, but is quickly rejected by Qiu Gao.

B While in BeiJing for sentencing, Zhi Yang meets Secretary Liang, a local official who is aware of Zhi Yang's reputation. Secretary Liang takes Zhi Yang under his wing, and entrusts him with important tasks.

11

I HATE TO NAG, BUT IT'S BEEN SLOW--

ALL RIGHT, ALL RIGHT!

MR. YANG, YOU'RE A MONTH LATE ON RENT.

GIVE ME TWO DAYS. YOU'LL GET YOUR MONEY.

13

SWORD FOR SALE!

FIGURES... JUST A FEW MONTHS AGO, I HAD PEOPLE BEGGING ME TO SELL THEM THIS SWORD. NOW I CAN'T *GIVE* IT AWAY.

COME ON, PEOPLE! WHO WANTS A NICE SWORD?

UH-OH. HERE COMES THE TIGER. RUN!

MOVE IT OR LOSE IT!

15

WHAT THE HELL ARE YOU STARING AT?

NEXT TIME, I'M TAKING YOUR EYEBALLS.

WHACK

The "tiger" in question was Er Niu, a local thug who went by the ironic name of "Hairless Tiger." He was the nephew of a local government official, which meant he was never punished for his antics.

FUP

GAH!

AMAZING!

HE DID IT!

PIPE DOWN OR LOSE YOUR TEETH! YOUR CHOICE.

≥ GULP ≤

SORRY.

THIS GUY HAS NO INTENTION OF BUYING THE SWORD. HE JUST WANTS TO PICK A FIGHT.

OKAY, SO IT CUTS COINS. WHAT DID YOU SAY ABOUT HAIR?

I SAID A HAIR FALLING ON THIS SWORD WOULD BE CUT IN HALF.

IT'S TEMPTING, BUT THE RISKS OUTWEIGH THE REWARDS.

FINE. LET'S SEE IF YOUR SECOND PLEDGE HOLDS UP.

WHOOH

WOW! RIGHT IN HALF.

ENOUGH! WHAT ABOUT THE THIRD BOAST?

SIGH... I SAID THIS SWORD COULD CUT A PERSON AND NOT GET BLOOD ON IT.

I CAN'T BE SATISFIED BY ONLY TWO OUT OF THREE.

INDEED, YOU ARE A HARD MAN TO CONVINCE.

FINE. PROVE IT! CUT DOWN ANY ONE OF THESE USELESS PEASANTS, AND I'LL BUY IT.

23

25

27

28

Zhi Yang accepted the ruling and sat in prison while they deliberated.

When word of Zhi Yang's actions and honorable surrender spread, public opinion of him rose. Many people visited him at the prison and brought him food and gifts. Meanwhile, Zhi Yang was ordered to appear before the chief commissioner in BeiJing for final sentencing.

ZHI YANG HAS CONDUCTED HIMSELF WITH HONOR SINCE THE KILLING.

MY LORDS, THE MAN YOU'RE ESCORTING TO BEIJING IS A HERO TO US. WE ASK THAT YOU TREAT HIM WELL ON THE JOURNEY.

AND HE DID US A FAVOR BY GETTING RID OF ER NIU.

I SAY WE GO EASY ON HIM.

DON'T WORRY. WE KNOW ALL ABOUT HIM.

Though the police escorts kept their word by not harming Zhi Yang, they left him little time for rest as they hurried to BeiJing.

The next day, Zhi Yang was brought before Secretary Liang in the Chief Commissioner's office. As it happened, the secretary was aware of the man before him.

WAIT, ZHI YANG?

THUD

DO THEY CALL YOU THE BLUE-FACED BEAST?

THEY DO, MY LORD.

Zhi Yang knew how lucky he was, and devoted himself to doing his new job well.

The effort didn't go unnoticed. In time, Zhi Yang was offered a promotion.

ZHI YANG, I'D LIKE TO MAKE YOU A COMMANDER IN THE LOCAL ARMY.

I THINK IT WOULD HELP IF YOU WERE TO DEMONSTRATE YOUR TALENTS. IT WOULD GO A LONG WAY TOWARD WINNING THE SUPPORT OF MY MEN.

OF COURSE, I DON'T KNOW IF YOU HAVE EXPERIENCE. AND THE OTHER OFFICERS MIGHT OBJECT.

THAT'S A GREAT IDEA! FETCH SOME ARMOR FOR ZHI YANG.

MY LORD.

MY LORD, YOU ARE TOO KIND TO MAKE SUCH AN OFFER. IN FACT, I WAS TRAINED IN MILITARY ARTS FROM A YOUNG AGE.

The next day, Secretary Liang summoned his commanders to a nearby arena for a martial arts demonstration.

WELCOME, MY LORD. AS ALWAYS, IT'S AN HONOR.

SOUND THE DRUM!

41

NYEH

YES, SIR!

CLOP CLOP

THONK

HOW ABOUT A MARTIAL ARTS DISPLAY?

YES, MY LORD!

HUP!

MY LORD! LIEUTENANT JIN ZHOU IS HERE TO DO YOUR BIDDING.

43

Zhi Yang donned the armor he'd been given before, grabbed the nearest spear, and charged into the arena.

FIGHT ME FOR MY RANK, WILL YOU? I'LL MAKE SURE THIS IS YOUR LAST SPARRING MATCH.

MY LORD, THIS IS AN EXHIBITION, NOT A FIGHT TO THE DEATH. LET'S REMOVE THE BLADES FROM THEIR SPEARS. OTHERWISE, THINGS COULD GET BAD VERY QUICKLY.

RIGHT. GOOD IDEA.

Da Wen ordered Zhi Yang and Jin Zhou to remove their blades and wrap the ends of their spears in fabric. Then they dipped the spear tips in lime powder. Whoever emerged with the fewest lime marks on him would be the winner.

NO NEED FOR INSULTS. HAVE A GOOD MATCH.

FUFF

READY, LITTLE MOUSE?

SAVE IT. I'M JUST GETTING WARMED UP!

HA!!!

CALL IT QUITS NOW, JIN ZHOU, AND THIS CAN ALL BE OVER.

WHUMP

HA! THE MATCH IS EVEN!

IS IT? WAIT, HOW?

FASTEST SPEAR STRIKE I'VE EVER SEEN.

COME ON, LIEUTENANT ZHOU! MAKE HIM REGRET THAT HE EVEN PUT ON THE ARMOR!

CAN'T... CAN'T FIGHT HIM OFF! DAMN IT!

NOW, YIELD.

AND LET'S CALL IT A DAY.

I DON'T BELIEVE IT.

STAND DOWN!

ZHI YANG IS THE VICTOR. AS AGREED EFORE THE BOUT, HE WILL NOW INHERIT JIN ZHOU'S RANK.

MY LORD, I MUST OBJECT TO YOUR RULING! JIN ZHOU'S EXPERTISE IS IN ARCHERY, NOT SPEARMANSHIP. LET HIM ATTEMPT TO REGAIN HIS RANK WITH AN ARCHERY CONTEST.

MY LORD! I WORRY THAT THEY'LL GET HURT BY THE ARROWS.

WILL YOU KNOCK IT OFF? WE'RE SOLDIERS! OF COURSE WE MIGHT GET HURT!

So Zhi Yang and Jin Zhou were both given bows and a quiver of arrows. The contest was to see who could hit the other.

TELL YOU WHAT: YOU CAN TAKE THE FIRST THREE SHOTS.

VERY WELL. AN ARCHERY CONTEST.

55

Up stepped General Suo Chao, whose skill as a fighter made up for his impulsive nature and short temper.

Suo Chao

LET HIM SPAR WITH ME, AND THEN DECIDE.

IT IS WELL KNOWN THAT JIN ZHOU HAS BEEN VERY ILL UNTIL RECENTLY. THE BOUT WAS UNFAIR!

IF ZHI YANG DEFEATS ME, THEN HE CAN HAVE MY RANK AS WELL. WHAT DO YOU SAY?

HMPH.

HE'S RIGHT. JIN ZHOU IS NOT IN TOP FORM. I SECOND SUO CHAO'S IDEA.

SIGH...IT'S CLEAR ZHI YANG WOULD BE A GOOD SOLDIER, AND STILL THEY RESIST. BUT HE MUST WIN THEM OVER.

IF THAT IS YOUR WILL, THEN YES.

SUO CHAO IS MORE DANGEROUS THAN JIN ZHOU. SO BE CAREFUL OUT THERE.

COME HERE, ZHI YANG.

WHAT SAY YOU? ARE YOU WILLING TO SPAR WITH SUO CHAO?

I'LL BRING YOU FRESH ARMOR TO CHANGE INTO AS WELL.

THANK YOU.

PFT.

SUO CHAO, I'M GIVING YOU A FRESH HORSE AND OUR FINEST ARMOR. TAKE THEM BOTH.

REMEMBER, EVEN THOUGH THE BOUT IS ONE-ON-ONE, YOU REPRESENT THE HONOR AND COURAGE OF US ALL.

GIVE IT A REST.

I'M JUST SAYING, DON'T BLOW IT.

READY? LET'S BEGIN!

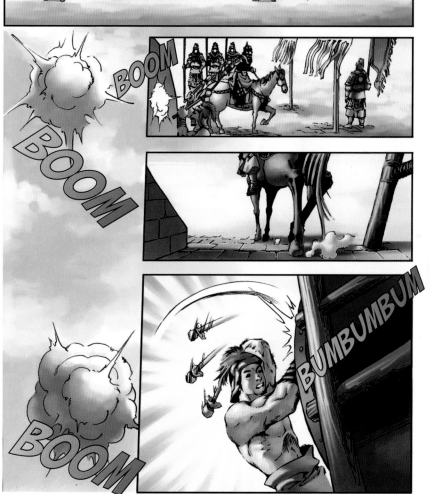

WHOA!

I'M GOING TO CHOP YOU DOWN LIKE A DAMNED OAK TREE!

IS YOUR BLADE AS DULL AS YOU ARE?

KLANG

CLOP CLOP CLOP

HAWHOOSH

73

LOOK AT THEM GO.

THIS MATCH WILL BE LEGENDARY!

INDEED. IT'S LIKE WATCHING TWO TIGERS FIGHT FOR THEIR LIVES.

IN ALL MY LONG YEARS ON THIS EARTH, I'VE NEVER WITNESSED A BOUT LIKE THIS!

YOU'RE ONLY 15, MORON.

WEAPONS UP! SECRETARY LIANG HAS CALLED A HALT TO THE MATCH. AT EASE, BOTH OF YOU.

THIS IS YOUR LUCKY DAY.

OH?

MY LORD.

MY LORD.

IT SEEMS ABSURD TO ALLOW THIS CONTEST TO GO ON ANY LONGER.

YOU HAVE BOTH DEMONSTRATED THAT YOU ARE EXTRAORDINARY SOLDIERS.

LUCKILY, THERE IS NO ACTUAL NEED TO REWARD ONE OF YOU WHILE PUNISHING THE OTHER.

THIS TRAY OF COINS IS YOURS TO SPLIT AS A REWARD FOR YOUR INCREDIBLE DISPLAY OF SKILL. AND I THINK THIS CALLS FOR A CELEBRATION. BEING OUT IN THIS SUN HAS MADE ME QUITE THIRSTY. I'M SURE IT'S WORSE FOR YOU UNDER ALL THAT ARMOR.

WE FIGHT ALONGSIDE ONE ANOTHER, AFTER ALL!

Secretary Liang's judgment was well received, and Zhi Yang was welcomed into the army's ranks.

WELL, ZHI YANG? WHAT DO YOU THINK?

EXCELLENT SWORDSMANSHIP, MY LORD. YOUR MOVES ARE AS SHARP AS YOUR BLADE.

HA HA HA! FLATTERY WILL GET YOU EVERYWHERE, YOU KNOW.

Time passed, and the spring came and went without incident.

One night, Secretary Liang and his wife were dining in celebration of the Dragon Boat Festival.

DARLING, DO YOU KNOW WHY WE ARE ABLE TO LIVE IN SUCH COMFORT AND SECURITY?

HOW COULD I FORGET, MY DEAR? YOU REMIND ME ALMOST EVERY SINGLE DAY.

HM. YOU SAY THAT, BUT IT SEEMS THAT YOU'VE FORGOTTEN HIS BIRTHDAY.

SIGH...NO, I DIDN'T. I'VE ALREADY SPENT A SMALL FORTUNE ON GIFTS FOR YOUR FATHER. I'LL SEND THEM SOON.

YOU TRIED THAT LAST YEAR, AND THE SHIPMENT WAS ROBBED.

SHENG GONGSUN

Chapter 2

The Benevolent Thief

Summary

When word got out of the caravan carrying Secretary Liang's gold, several outlaws in the area took notice. Tang Liu, also known as the Red Devil, was one of them. Upon learning of the gold shipment, he sought out a partnership with Gai Chao of DongQi, a known benefactor and sympathizer with the destitute. When Tang Liu is captured by a local patrol, he is brought to Gai Chao, who convinces the constable to release the prisoner. Upon learning of the gold shipment from Tang Liu, Gai Chao begins planning a robbery and sends Yong Wu, a trusted friend, to recruit the Ruan brothers, local fishermen who've fallen on hard times and will be useful allies. When another man, a guru named Sheng Gongsun, arrives with a similar plan to steal the gold, the seven men finalize their plan and prepare themselves for the coming heist.

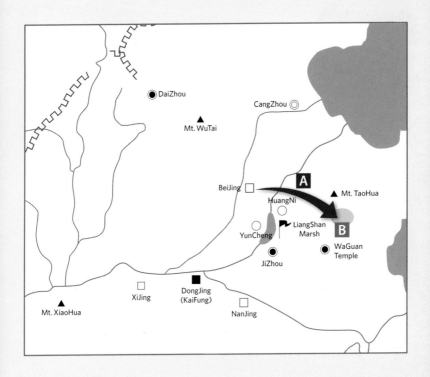

A Secretary Liang dispatches a caravan carrying 100,000 gold coins. The purpose of the caravan is to seek out and purchase birthday gifts for Secretary Liang's father-in-law. When word of the shipment gets out, local bandits like Tang Liu take notice.

B Gai Chao, Tang Liu, Yong Wu, the Ruan brothers, and Shen Gongsun plot to steal the gold when it passes near the village of DongQi.

In the district of ShanDong, a local magistrate named WenBin Shi received orders to investigate the mysterious group of bandits gathering in LiangShan Marsh.

WenBin Shi immediately summoned his security council to devise a strategy for dealing with the apparent threat.

BRING IN HENG LEI AND TONG ZHU.

MY LORD!

HENG LEI AND TONG ZHU, REPORTING FOR DUTY, MY LORD.

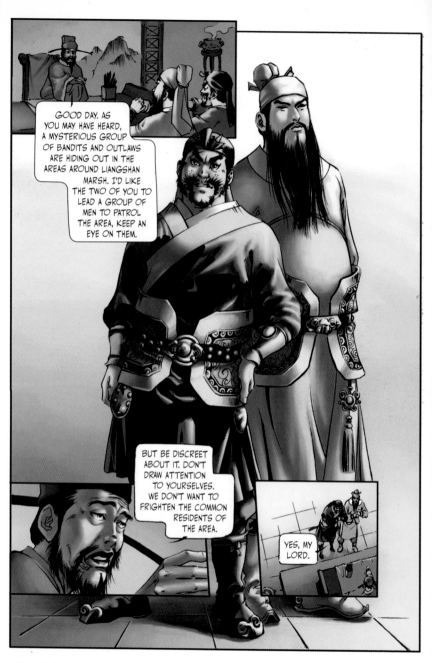

GOOD DAY. AS YOU MAY HAVE HEARD, A MYSTERIOUS GROUP OF BANDITS AND OUTLAWS ARE HIDING OUT IN THE AREAS AROUND LIANGSHAN MARSH. I'D LIKE THE TWO OF YOU TO LEAD A GROUP OF MEN TO PATROL THE AREA, KEEP AN EYE ON THEM.

BUT BE DISCREET ABOUT IT. DON'T DRAW ATTENTION TO YOURSELVES. WE DON'T WANT TO FRIGHTEN THE COMMON RESIDENTS OF THE AREA.

YES, MY LORD.

On their first night of patrol, Heng Lei's men came to the village of DongQi.

TEMPLE'S OPEN AWFULLY LATE.

IT SHOULDN'T BE. SOMETHING ISN'T RIGHT HERE. GO INSIDE AND CHECK IT OUT.

KREAK

ZZZ, ZZZ

WONDERFUL. LOOKS LIKE WE'VE GOT A VAGRANT. AND PROBABLY A THIEF.

After clearing out the temple, Heng Lei and his patrol came to the manor of the local chief Gai Chao. Gai Chao was the richest man in DongQi, but also a generous benefactor who sympathized most with those who had the least. He respected officials, but not necessarily the office.

THIS WAS A LONG FIRST NIGHT. I DON'T KNOW ABOUT YOU, BUT I'M STARVING. LET'S SEE IF GAI CHAO HAS ANY FOOD.

TAP TAP TAP

WHO IS IT?

CONSTABLE HENG LEI.

AT THIS HOUR?

MY LORD, SOMEONE'S HERE TO SEE YOU.

THOUGHT YOU'D LIKE TO KNOW WE CAPTURED A THIEF FROM ONE OF THE LOCAL TEMPLES.

GOOD EVENING. WHAT BRINGS YOU HERE AT THIS TIME OF NIGHT?

YOU DID? THAT'S WONDERFUL TO HEAR.

MY LORD, I WAS ASSIGNED TO PATROL THIS AREA BY THE LOCAL MAGISTRATE, AND TONIGHT IS OUR FIRST PATROL.

97

I THINK I'D LIKE TO MEET THIS "THIEF" HE CAUGHT.

AHEM.

MY LORD?

SEE IF HENG LI WANTS ANOTHER ROUND. I'LL BE RIGHT BACK.

YES, MY LORD.

MORE WINE?

99

SO TELL ME, THIEF: WHAT'S YOUR BUSINESS IN DONGQI?

LET ME GUESS: HIS NAME GAI CHAO.

WHY ARE YOU LOOKING FOR HIM?

LET'S JUST SAY I KNOW HOW TO MAKE HIM RICH.

I'M NOT A THIEF! I'M JUST LOOKING FOR SOMEONE.

VERY WELL. WHO ARE YOU LOOKING FOR?

A LOCAL MAN, KNOWN TO BE GENEROUS AND SYMPATHETIC TO THE DESTITUTE.

IT IS. WHY? DO YOU KNOW THIS MAN? HOW CAN I FIND HIM?

HM. WELL, MY FRIEND, THIS IS YOUR LUCKY DAY...

101

103

HUH? THAT WASN'T SUPPOSED TO HAPPEN.

GENTLEMEN, THE THIEF YOU CAUGHT IS ACTUALLY A RELATIVE OF MINE. HE USED TO LIVE HERE WITH HIS MOTHER, MY SISTER. BUT THEY MOVED TO NANJING WHEN HE WAS ONLY A SMALL BOY.

THEN WHY DID THEY ARREST YOU?

BUT WHY DID YOU BECOME A THIEF? WHY NOT JUST ASK ME FOR HELP?

MY LORD, WAIT! HE'S NOT LYING.

I SWEAR, IF YOU'VE BROUGHT DISGRACE ON THIS FAMILY, I'LL FLOG YOU MYSELF!

I'M NOT A THIEF. I NEVER ACTUALLY STOLE ANYTHING!

105

YOU ARE MOST KIND. PLEASE FORGIVE MY NEPHEW.

MY LORD, IF I'D KNOWN IT WAS YOUR NEPHEW, WE'D HAVE LET HIM SLEEP IT OFF IN THE TEMPLE.

CONSTABLE, COME INSIDE WITH ME FOR A MOMENT. I HAVE SOMETHING FOR YOU.

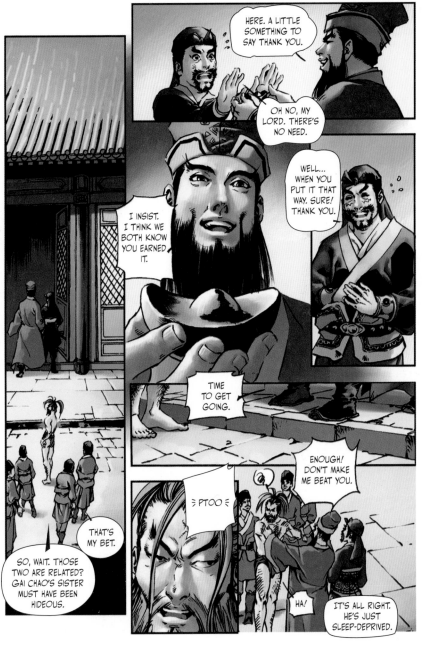

APOLOGIES AGAIN. HE MAY BE THE SIZE OF AN APE, BUT HE'S CLEARLY STILL JUST A CHILD. I'LL SEE HE DOESN'T BOTHER YOU.

NO BOTHER AT ALL! SORRY TO HAVE TROUBLED YOU.

Once Heng Li and his patrolmen left, Gai Chao had a chance to sit down with his hulking guest…

ALL RIGHT, IT'S JUST THE TWO OF US NOW. TIME FOR YOU TO START TELLING ME ABOUT YOURSELF. LET'S START WITH YOUR NAME.

MY NAME IS TANG LIU, MY LORD. I'M SURE IT WON'T SURPRISE YOU, BASED ON MY APPEARANCE, THAT I AM KNOWN AS RED DEVIL.

AND I HAVE A PLAN FOR MAKING YOU WEALTHIER THAN YOU ALREADY ARE.

I'D BE ROTTING IN JAIL NOW IF IT WASN'T FOR YOU.

IT'S THE LEAST I CAN DO AFTER YOU BAILED ME OUT OF TROUBLE WITH THE PATROL.

PLEASE, DON'T BOW.

111

But Tang Liu was so agitated that he could not sleep. So he grabbed a nearby sword and went chasing after Heng Lei and his men.

THA

COME BACK HERE, YOU THIEVING BASTARDS!!!

THMP THMP THMP

WHAT THE...?

119

121

The man who broke up the fight was a local resident named Yong Wu, a benevolent man known for his profound intelligence and wisdom.

WHO IS THIS MAN WHO CROSSES SWORDS WITH CONSTABLE HENG LEI?

IF YOU CAN BELIEVE IT, THIS INBRED HALF-WIT IS GAI CHAO'S NEPHEW.

HE IS?

LISTEN, YOU BLUBBERING IMBECILE. THAT MONEY IS *MINE*. IT WAS *GIVEN* TO ME BY YOUR UNCLE. I DON'T OWE YOU A *DAMN THING!*

AND YOU'RE NOTHING BUT A THIEF DISGUISED AS AN OFFICIAL. GIVE ME THE MONEY!

YOUNG MAN, PUT DOWN YOUR SWORD. YOUR BEHAVIOR WILL DO NOTHING BUT HURT YOUR UNCLE'S HONOR.

I HAD NO IDEA GAI CHAO HAD A NEPHEW.

LISTEN TO THE MAN! HE'S TALKING SENSE!

BACK OFF! I WON'T DISGRACE MY UNCLE ANY MORE THAN THE MAN WHO STOLE MONEY FROM HIM!

GIVE IT BACK, OR SO HELP ME YOU'LL PAY IT BACK WITH YOUR LIFE!

I'VE HAD ENOUGH OF YOUR MOUTH. THINK I'LL JAM MY SWORD DOWN IT!

ENOUGH! STOP THIS, BOTH OF YOU!

GO AHEAD! GIVE IT A SHOT.

MY LORD! IT'S GAI CHAO!

I WILL ENJOY KILLING YOU!

YOU WOULD, TYRANT!

SIGH. DOES THE LAW FORBID LETTING THEM KILL EACH OTHER?

NEPHEW! WHAT IS THE MEANING OF THIS? I THOUGHT I TOLD YOU TO BEHAVE YOURSELF.

WHY ARE YOU HARASSING CONSTABLE HENG LEI? HE'S A GOOD MAN.

TELL YOUR LITTLE SNOT NEPHEW THAT YOU GAVE ME MONEY BEFORE!

MAYBE THEN HE'LL BACK THE HELL OFF!

NEPHEW, IS THIS ABOUT MONEY? HOW DARE YOU...

GO HOME AND BATHE. NOW!

FINE!

I'M SO SORRY. HIS MOTHER WAS NUTS TOO.

I THOUGHT AS MUCH.

OF COURSE, STEALING A FORTUNE IS NOT THE WORK OF ONE MAN. IT TAKES SEVERAL.

I MET HIM LAST NIGHT. HIS NAME IS TANG LIU. HE WAS ARRESTED FOR LOITERING, BUT IN FACT HE WAS LOOKING FOR ME. TURNS OUT, HE WANTS TO STEAL A FORTUNE.

I CAN RECOMMEND A FEW PEOPLE, IF YOU'D LIKE.

WHO DID YOU HAVE IN MIND?

I HAVE THREE SPECIFIC PEOPLE IN MIND. BROTHERS. ALL STRONG MARTIAL ARTISTS. ALL LOYAL.

OH? TELL ME ABOUT THESE THREE BROTHERS.

HA HA HA! I THOUGHT AS MUCH. BANDITS ARE NOTHING IF NOT PREDICTABLE.

IT WOULD BE QUICKER IF I ASKED THEM IN PERSON.

THEIR LAST NAME IS RUAN. FIRST NAMES XIAOER, XIAOWU, AND XIAOQI. THEY'RE FISHERMEN BY TRADE, AND THEY LIVE DOWN IN THE VILLAGE OF SHIJIE.

AH, YES. I'VE HEARD OF THESE THREE. SHIJIE ISN'T THAT FAR FROM HERE. WHY DON'T YOU SEND SOMEONE TO FETCH THEM?

Without further delay, Yong Wu rode through the night to the village of ShiJie and sought out the Ruan brothers.

131

WELL, I WAS HOPING YOU COULD FIND ME SOME LARGE CARP. I'M THROWING A PARTY.

HEH. GOOD LUCK WITH THAT. THERE ARE NO BIG FISH HERE. THEY ALL GATHER IN LIANGSHAN MARSH.

OKAY. WHY DON'T YOU GO THERE TO FISH?

WE USED TO, BUT...

WHAT? WHAT'S THE MATTER?

WELL, WE USED TO FISH IN LIANGSHAN MARSH ALL THE TIME. IT'S HOW WE MADE ALL OUR MONEY.

BUT A FEW YEARS BACK, THE AREA WAS TAKEN OVER BY A GROUP OF BANDITS, SO WE DON'T BOTHER GOING NEAR THERE ANYMORE.

WHAT KIND OF BANDITS ARE THEY?

THE PROFESSIONAL KIND. THEIR LEADER IS NONE OTHER THAN LUN WANG.

YES...

HIS THREE LIEUTENANTS ARE QIAN DU, WAN SONG, AND GUI ZHU.

AND JUST RECENTLY, THEY ADDED A FOURTH LIEUTENANT--NONE OTHER THAN CHONG LIN, WHOSE SKILLS IN BATTLE ARE ALREADY LEGENDARY.

THEY'VE COMPLETELY TAKEN OVER LIANGSHAN MARSH. AND WE'VE LOST OUR SOURCE OF INCOME.

DESPERATION. THESE BROTHERS ARE ALMOST TOO EASY TO CONVINCE.

INDEED. WHAT DO YOU SAY TO ANOTHER ROUND?

I SAY ≡HKUP≡ YES, PLEASE.

HA HA! POUR, THEN!

HAVE YOU EVER THOUGHT ABOUT FIGHTING THE LIANGSHAN BANDITS?

NO WAY! TOO MANY PEOPLE SUPPORT THEIR CAUSE.

WHY NOT TRY TO JOIN THEM, THEN?

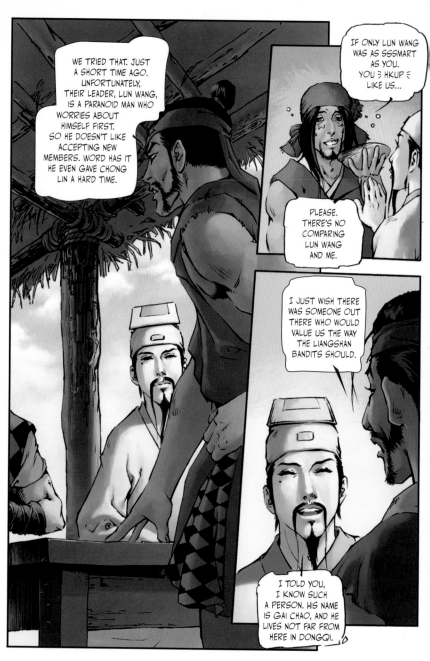

WE TRIED THAT. JUST A SHORT TIME AGO. UNFORTUNATELY, THEIR LEADER, LUN WANG, IS A PARANOID MAN WHO WORRIES ABOUT HIMSELF FIRST. SO HE DOESN'T LIKE ACCEPTING NEW MEMBERS. WORD HAS IT HE EVEN GAVE CHONG LIN A HARD TIME.

IF ONLY LUN WANG WAS AS SSSMART AS YOU. YOU ≋ HKUP ≋ LIKE US...

PLEASE. THERE'S NO COMPARING LUN WANG AND ME.

I JUST WISH THERE WAS SOMEONE OUT THERE WHO WOULD VALUE US THE WAY THE LIANGSHAN BANDITS SHOULD.

I TOLD YOU, I KNOW SUCH A PERSON. HIS NAME IS GAI CHAO, AND HE LIVES NOT FAR FROM HERE IN DONGQI.

GAI CHAO? I'VE HEARD HIS NICKNAME BEFORE. SOMETHING ABOUT A PAGODA.

PERHAPS, BUT THE ONLY PROBLEM IS THAT WE'VE NEVER MET HIM.

HE'S NOT HARD TO FIND IF THERE'S A REASON TO MEET HIM.

THE NICKNAME DOESN'T DO HIM JUSTICE. HE IS A GREAT MAN, AND HE CAN SET THINGS RIGHT FOR YOU.

YOU CAN TELL HIM WE'D LAY OUR LIVES DOWN FOR A CHANCE AT A GOOD LIFE.

I WILL.

HERE'S THE IDEA. ONCE MORE: IT'S NOT EASY.

PLEASE THANK HIM FOR EVEN CONSIDERING OUR SERVICE.

SECRETARY LIANG IN BEIJING HAS DISPATCHED A CARAVAN TO BUY GIFTS FOR HIS FATHER. IT'S CARRYING 100,000 GOLD PIECES.

GAI CHAO HAS BEEN WORKING WITH A MAN NAMED TANG LIU TO FORMULATE A PLAN FOR STEALING THE MONEY. AND I WANT THE THREE OF YOU TO HELP US DO IT.

WELL, WE HAVE VERY LITTLE TIME TO LOSE. I SUGGEST YOU ALL SET OUT WITH ME FIRST THING IN THE MORNING.

IS EVERYONE AWAKE AND SOBERED UP?

Yong Wu spent the night at the brothers' home, and in the morning they were on their way to meet with Gai Chao.

Back in DongQi…

LOOK! GAO CHAI HAS COME TO MEET US IN PERSON.

MY LORD, YOUR REPUTATION IS WITHOUT EQUAL. SHOULD YOU ACCEPT US, WE'D SERVE YOU WITHOUT HESITATION.

HA! YOUR FLATTERY IS KIND, BUT UNCALLED FOR.

So Gai Chao and the three brothers pledged an oath of fidelity and swore to carry out the heist no matter what.

SECRETARY LIANG IS A MAN WHO GETS RICH OFF THE BROKEN BACKS OF THE PEOPLE.

FINE. YOU'RE A TOTAL BUM. BUT A GENEROUS ONE!

ON BEHALF OF THEM, WE PLEDGE TO RESTORE A BIT OF BALANCE.

HA HA HA!!!

The six newly sworn brothers celebrated their pledge through the night and into the next day.

MY LORD, SOMEONE TO SEE YOU.

NOT NOW!

CAN'T YOU SEE WE'RE CELEBRATING SOMETHING IMPORTANT?

GIVE HIM SOME RICE AND SEND HIM ON HIS WAY.

I DID GIVE HIM SOME RICE. BUT HE REFUSES TO LEAVE AND DEMANDS TO SEE YOU.

KREAK

MY LORD!!!

HE WON'T BE PLACATED BY RICE, HUH? FINE!

GIVE HIM SOME MEAT.

159

163

165

So Gai Chao introduced Sheng GongSun to Tang Liu and the Ruan brothers.

Gai Chao sat in the head chair, and the others took their place to either side of him.

I KNOW A MAN WHO LIVES NEAR THERE NAMED SHENG BAI. HE OWES ME A FAVOR.

WE'LL USE HIS HOUSE AS A BASE.

ALREADY AHEAD OF YOU. THEY'RE COMING BY WAY OF HUANGNIGANG ROAD.

LET'S BEGIN. IF WE'RE GOING TO INTERCEPT THIS SHIPMENT OF GOLD, WE MUST FIRST FIGURE OUT EXACTLY WHICH ROUTE THE CARAVAN IS TAKING.

AH, THAT'S PERFECT!

While Gai Chao and Yong Wu worked out the details of their scheme, the seven bandits spent their time preparing for the day of the heist.

Meanwhile, many miles away but creeping ever closer to HuangNiGang under a scorching summer sun, was the caravan carrying Secretary Liang's gold. A caravan led by none other than the Blue-Faced Beast, Zhi Yang.

LET'S TAKE A REST HERE. JUST FOR A MOMENT...

CAN'T...CAN'T KEEP THIS UP. TOO DAMNED HOT.

≋ HUFF, HUFF ≋

MUST SIT DOWN. CAN'T TAKE ANOTHER STEP.

KEEP MOVING! THIS PLACE IS CRAWLING WITH BANDITS. YOU SIT, YOU DIE!

AH...MUCH BETTER.

The Zero-Sum Game

The plight of Zhi Yang following his expulsion from civil service, when considered alongside the story of Gai Chao hatching a plan to rob a fortune from Secretary Liang, provides an insightful glimpse into the contrasting realities of life during the Song Dynasty. For those who live close to the central cities, and therefore live under the influence of civil and governing institutions, there is a sense that common purpose can be a civic ideal that overcomes a winner-take-all mentality. But in the fairly lawless hinterlands of rural China, where the influence of these institutions is barely acknowledged, much less felt, there is no such common purpose, and life is an endless parade of one person building him- or herself up by knocking someone else down.

When Zhi Yang is brought before Secretary Liang's army for a demonstration of his talents, the ground rules are made clear: in order for him to achieve a rank, someone already in the army must be supplanted. This rule seems more in line with ancient tradition than current sentiment, though, and soon Secretary Liang discovers that his soldiers strenuously object to Zhi Yang's appointment, not because they don't accept him as a viable soldier – it's clear that he is well-trained in martial arts – but because it must come at the expense of someone else's position. Secretary Liang slowly realizes this, and then it occurs to him that the purpose of the army is larger than simply competing for positions. Why should he merely trade one good soldier for another when having two good soldiers would strengthen the army and make them more effective? As the man in charge of the army in BeiJing, Secretary Liang realizes the higher importance of the common good, and promotes both Zhi Yang and his competitor. Why should one man have to lose when everyone gains from both men winning?

Compare this to the story of Gai Chao and the multiple thieves who come to him asking for sponsorship as they plot to steal Secretary Liang's gold. DongQi village, despite being not far from BeiJing by today's standards, might as well be a million miles from there for all the ways it differs: men can be arrested simply for being suspicious, local officials are easily bribed, and there is no individual or agency that can be relied on to look after the well-being of others. (This is what makes Gai Chao such a popular man: He helps people when others won't.) When such conditions are the stuff of everyday life, it's easy to see why a man wouldn't think about or believe in the common good, and instead believe that the only way to get ahead in life is by taking from someone else. Gai Chao is sympathetic to those who endure this reality, and while he does not seem to despise Secretary Liang for his wealth, he is more than willing to help those who'd like to relieve him of it.

Zhi Yang and Gai Chao live in the same land at the same time, but their life experiences couldn't be more different: Zhi Yang is the beneficiary of a social order that leaves room for fairness in the name of the common good, while for Gai Chao life is nothing more than a zero-sum game, where one man's wealth is another man's poverty.

TALES FROM CHINA

OUTLAWS of the MARSH

Vol. 01

Vol. 02

Vol. 03

Vol. 04

Vol. 05

Vol. 06

Vol. 07

Vol. 08

Vol. 09

Vol. 10

Vol. 11

Vol. 12

Vol. 13

Vol. 14

Vol. 15

Vol. 16

Vol. 17

Vol. 18

Vol. 19

Vol. 20